Five True Dog Stories

by MARGARET DAVIDSON

Pictures by SUSANNE SUBA

SCHOLASTIC BOOK SERVICES

NEW YORK · TORONTO · LONDON · AUCKLAND · SYDNEY · TOKYO

Especially for Patrick

Text copyright © 1977 by Margaret Davidson. Illustrations copyright © 1977 by Scholastic Magazines, Inc. All rights reserved. Published by Scholastic Book Services, a division of Scholastic Magazines, Inc.

12 11 10 9 8 7 6 5 4 3 2 1   2   7 8 9/7 0 1 2/8

Printed in the U.S.A.

Contents

Dox,
the greatest dog detective in the world

The policeman just happened to be passing a pet store one day. He looked in and saw a roly-poly German shepherd pup in the window. And the pup looked back at him. The man wasn't even thinking of buying a dog. But a few minutes later he came out of the shop with the dog in his arms. "It was love at first

sight," Giovanni Maimone told his friends. And he named his new pet Dox.

Maimone worked as a policeman in the city of Turin, Italy. He decided to train Dox to help him in his work. Dox was a very smart dog. And he, like most dogs, had a good sense of smell. Maimone wanted to train Dox to find hidden things — jewels or money or people.

Maimone worked with Dox as much as he could. First he took a handkerchief and a cigarette case. They both belonged to someone Dox didn't know. And they carried the person's own special smell. Maimone hid the cigarette case behind the cushion of a big overstuffed chair. He let Dox sniff the handkerchief. "Find it, boy!" he said.

Of course Dox didn't understand — not at first. So Maimone led the dog to the overstuffed chair. He lifted the cushion — and there was the cigarette case. Dox sniffed at it. "Good boy!" Maimone said — as if Dox had found it by himself.

Very soon Dox understood exactly what was going on. Every time his master asked him to sniff something and then said, "Find it!" Dox knew he must find something that smelled the same.

Of course it was still just a game they were playing. Then one day a jewelry store was robbed. The thief escaped with many fine jewels. He'd left nothing behind — except a dirty old glove. Mai-

mone decided to take Dox along. It was time to test the dog on a real case.

When they got to the jewelry store, several other policemen were already there. One looked up and said with a grin, "Oh, I see you've brought Dox. Do you think he can lend us a paw?"

Everyone laughed. Everyone except Maimone. Quietly he asked for the glove. He let Dox sniff it. Then he said, "Find him, Dox!"

First Dox sniffed across the floor of the jewelry store. Out the door he ran, followed by Maimone and several other policemen. Dox moved slowly but steadily for several blocks. Then he came to a big highway. He started down it one way. He stopped. The busy highway was filled with so many smells — gasoline fumes and grass and rubber tires and trees. How could he possibly smell the special glove smell?

But he did. Dox sniffed by the side of the road for a minute or two. Then he set off in the other direction. He never lost the trail again. At last he turned off the highway into a narrow side street. Dox led the men to one of the houses on the street and sat down on the porch.

Maimone knocked on the door. His knock was answered by a woman with a baby in her arms. "What do you want?" she snapped.

The policemen explained. "There's no one here," she answered. "Except for *her*...." She jiggled the baby in her arms. "My husband's in jail."

But Maimone was still suspicious. After all, Dox had led them right to this house. He and the other policemen kept checking. They soon found out that the woman was lying. Her husband *had* been in jail. But now he was out. A few days later the police caught him in a nearby town. He soon admitted that he had robbed the jewelry store. Then he had gone home for a few minutes to say good-bye to his wife and child.

Dox had solved his first case!

So the career of Dox, the dog detective, began. Before long the police in other towns heard about Dox. Often they asked for his help. He worked with the police all over Italy.

Other people knew the big dog too. Some of Dox's best friends were restaurant owners. On his birthday he could eat all he wanted in any one of their restaurants — free.

Maimone would lead him from one place to another. At each door Dox would stop and sniff. He'd move on until he found one that seemed to have nicer smells than all the rest. Then he would

go in for his favorite birthday dinner of spaghetti and pork.

On Dox's thirteenth birthday Maimone led him from restaurant to restaurant as usual. Dox seemed to be having an especially hard time deciding this year. "Choose, will you?" Maimone finally begged. "*I'm* getting hungry."

Just then they came to a small restaurant. Dox took a deep sniff. He became very still. Only his nose continued to twitch. He quickly pushed open the door and went inside.

But Dox wasn't interested in food. Not now. He headed straight for a man

who was sitting at a small corner table. The man kept on shoveling food into his mouth. He tried very hard to pretend he didn't see Dox. It was no use. Maimone recognized the man right away. He was a criminal who had escaped from the police. He was caught now — because Dox had remembered his human smell for more than *six* years.

Year after year Dox did his job. In fifteen years he helped catch more than 400 criminals!

"He has probably cracked more cases than any detective on the force," one police officer said. "We consider him one of our best men."

Grip,
the dog who was a thief

Grip was a friendly dog. And a friendly dog was just what Tom Gerrard wanted — for Tom Gerrard was a thief. He lived in the city of London, England, more than 300 years ago. Sometimes Tom Gerrard robbed big homes and stores. But most of all he liked to steal from people. That's what he trained Grip to do — to pick people's pockets.

First the man and the dog hid in an alley near a busy London street. And they waited. They waited until a man came by — a well-dressed man who might be carrying a lot of money.

Tom pointed at the man and softly snapped his fingers. Grip trotted out of the alley and began a happy dog's dance in front of the man.

He frisked, he wriggled, he wagged his tail. Sometimes the man just pushed past. But most people stopped to pet the friendly dog.

This was just what Grip had been waiting for. He would continue to prance and wriggle. But he was also using his nose to sniff out the smell of leather — the smell of a purse full of money.

It never took Grip long to find what he was looking for. Then his big mouth would open and close over the pocket with the purse in it. And with one powerful tug he'd tear the pocket *and* the purse away from the man's clothes!

Then Grip would dash away — leaving the man standing openmouthed. "Hey, you! Stop!" the man usually shouted. And the chase would begin.

Some of the men could run very fast. But Grip was never caught. He knew just where to go. He knew all the twisting streets and narrow alleys of London. He'd race up one and down another. Sometimes he would hide in a dark doorway until the man ran by. Then Grip would come out — and run the other way!

Grip always kept running until he was sure he was safe. Finally, with the purse still held firmly in his teeth, he would go back to the first alley where his master was waiting for him.

"Good dog, Grip!" Tom Gerrard always said as the dog dropped the purse into his hand. These few words of praise were all the reward Grip worked for.

What a team they made — the thief and the dog. Probably Tom Gerrard could have gone on stealing for many more years — if he'd been content just to pick pockets.

But Tom was a greedy man. One raw

and windy winter night he stopped a stagecoach on a road outside town. The door of the coach burst open. Three men with guns jumped out. Tom didn't stand a chance. He was captured and thrown into jail.

Poor Grip. For the next few weeks he wandered about the streets of London. The only food he ate was bits of garbage. And he slept in doorways or dirty alleys.

Then one day Grip saw a man walking down the street. He trotted up to him — and the man patted his head.

That was all the lonely dog needed. He followed the man home.

But who was this man Grip had chosen to be his next master? Was he another thief, like Tom Gerrard? Not at all. The man he picked to be his new master turned out to be the minister of a church instead!

Wolf,
the dog who saved other dogs

Wolf was not a friendly dog. He loved his master and mistress very much. But he didn't like other people. Wolf didn't seem to like other dogs either. He hardly ever played with the other collies that lived with him at Sunnybank Farm.

Wolf didn't like other dogs much, but he seemed to feel he had to take care of them. A big sign at the beginning of the farm's long, curving driveway read: "GO SLOW! DOGS RUNNING FREE!" Still, cars and trucks often would come roaring up the driveway.

Once a litter of pups chose the middle of the drive as their playground. So for hours at a time poor Wolf lay on the grass nearby. He watched the puppies race and tumble up and down the driveway. Every time he heard a car turn in from the road he got up and circled round and round the pups until they were in a tight bunch. Then he herded them off the drive.

But Wolf couldn't watch the puppies all the time. One day they were playing in the driveway as usual. A delivery truck turned into the farm. It swept around the first curve and came racing toward the pups.

Just then Wolf came out of a clump of trees across the lawn. He saw the danger the puppies were in. But the truck was coming so fast! And he was too far away to get them out of the way in time!

Wolf began to bark. He dashed a little

way toward the dogs. Still barking, he swung around and raced toward the trees again.

"Come on everyone! Chase me!" his loud bark seemed to be saying. And one after another the puppies did run after Wolf — off the driveway and away from the truck.

So the years passed peacefully at Sunnybank Farm. Wolf continued to watch over dogs who couldn't take care of themselves. The rest of the time he went his own way.

Wolf especially liked to take long walks. One warm spring afternoon he took a walk that led him to a railroad track.

Wolf knew about roads and cars. He also knew about railroad tracks and trains. He always stopped before crossing any railroad track. He would look in both directions and listen hard. Then he crossed quickly to the other side.

He did this now. He looked left and then right. He cocked his head. There was no train to be seen. But Wolf sat down to wait anyway. He must have heard the sound of a whistle in the distance.

A little brown dog walked past Wolf. The dog didn't look. He didn't listen either. He just walked onto the tracks and sat down to scratch a few fleas.

Wolf sprang up. He barked in warning. The dog just went on scratching. Then the sound of the train's whistle came again — much louder this time. And the train swept into sight!

Finally the little brown dog looked up. But *still* he didn't move. Now Wolf jumped and threw himself against the little dog. The dog flew through the air and landed in a nearby ditch.

Wolf tried to leap into the ditch too. He almost made it. But not quite. A piece of metal on the engine hit the side of his head. Wolf lay by the tracks. The dog who didn't even like other dogs very much would never move again. He had given his life to save a stranger.

Wolf's owner was a famous writer named Alfred Payson Terhune. Mr. Terhune wrote many more stories about Wolf and the other collies who lived at Sunnybank Farm. You can find these stories in your library.

Barry,
the dog who saved people

Today fine roads lead over the high
mountains of Switzerland. Snow plows
keep the roads open even in the worst
weather. But it wasn't always this way.

Before the roads were built it was
often very hard to cross over the mountains in winter. The only way was
through some of the passes — pathways
between the high peaks. One of these
passes was called the Great St. Bernard
Pass. At the highest point of the pass
stood a big stone building. This was the
monastery of Great St. Bernard. Monks
had lived here for hundreds of years.

They helped people travel safely in the mountains.

Sometimes the monks led travelers along the narrow path through the pass. And sometimes, when wild storms raged, they searched for those who might be lost.

This could be very dangerous work. But the monks had help. A group of big, shaggy dogs called St. Bernards also lived at the monastery. This is the story of one of those dogs. Barry was his name.

Barry was born in the spring of 1800. At first he romped and rolled with his brothers and sisters. He tagged after the bigger dogs. And he ate and slept whenever he felt like it.

But soon the short mountain summer was over. The first snow fell. It was time for Barry and the other young St. Bernards to go to school. They had some very important lessons to learn.

First Barry had to learn to obey. He learned to come when the monks called

him, to sit and lie down when the monks
told him to. He learned how to walk in
the deep snow. He learned how to turn
his big paws outward — and spread the
pads of his paws to keep from sinking in
the snow. At first he still sank in up to
his belly. But after a while he could
walk on the snowy crust without breaking through.

Now it was time for harder lessons.
Barry learned to lead people through the
pass even when the narrow path was
buried under many feet of snow. And he
learned one of the hardest lessons of all
— to find people who might be lost in a
storm.

If the person could walk, Barry led
him back to the monastery. But sometimes a person would be hurt — or
weakened by the cold. Then Barry raced
back to the monastery to lead the monks
back to the spot.

He also learned to search for people
who were lost *under* the snow. Sometimes an avalanche — a great slide of

snow — would break free from one of the high peaks. It would come crashing down the mountain and bury anyone who was in its path.

The dogs were especially important at times like this. A dog could smell people even when they were buried under the snow. Then he would bark loudly, and the monks would come running.

All winter Barry and the other dogs learned their lessons. And before long the monks began to watch Barry very carefully. There was something special about the dog. He learned much faster than the others. But that was not enough. Would Barry also be brave? Could the monks trust him as a rescue dog?

At last the lessons were over, and Barry went to work. One afternoon he was trotting ahead of a long line of workmen, leading them through the pass. There was a loud booming noise. It was the beginning of an avalanche!

Barry had never heard this sound before. But somehow he knew that something terrible was about to happen. He raced ahead, barking. Then he circled back around the men. He was trying to get them to move faster. And the men tried. But the last three didn't make it. Moments later the avalanche rolled down over the trail — and the three men were buried under it.

They were probably still alive. It is possible to breathe under snow, but not for long.

Barry looked at the snowy spot for a moment. Then he bounded away. A few minutes later he dashed into the court-yard of the monastery. The monks came running when they heard his frantic barks. *"It's trouble I can't handle alone!"* those barks meant. *"Follow me!"* Then he started out into the snow again.

The monks followed Barry back to where the avalanche had slid across the path. And the men who had gotten through safely told them what had happened.

"Find them, Barry," a monk ordered.

Barry began to sniff across the snow. Suddenly he barked. One of the monks ran over. Carefully he poked a long pole down into the snow. Nothing. He moved a few feet and poked again. Still nothing. So he tried a third time — and gave a shout. "Here!"

Other monks began to dig. A few minutes later the man was free. He was shivering and blue with cold, but he was alive! Soon the other two men were saved too.

That night everyone — the monks and the rescued men — made a big fuss over Barry. They praised him. They petted him. They gave him a large bowl of juicy meat scraps. And the monks nodded to one another. They had been right. This was going to be a *very* special dog.

One day Barry was out on patrol. He saw a small mound of snow. Something was sticking out of that mound — something that looked like the end of a red scarf. Barry raced over. He saw now that the mound was a little girl! She lay

curled up in the snow. Barry poked her.
Was she still alive? She was. But the
cold had made her very weak and sleepy.

Once more Barry seemed to know just
what to do. He didn't run back to the
monastery this time. He lay down beside
the little girl instead. He half covered
her with his warm, furry body. And he
began to lick her face with his big, rough
tongue.

At first the girl didn't move. But
slowly as she grew warmer she began
to stir. She snuggled under Barry's belly.
And she opened her eyes.

She wasn't frightened. She knew right away the big dog was a friend. She continued to snuggle close to his side — and slowly his warmth woke her up. But she was still too weak to stand.

Barry looked around. It was very cold now. But when the sun went down it would be much, much colder.

Barry tugged at the girl's coat. He stood up. He lay down beside her again. It was as if he were telling her something. And maybe he was. Because now the little girl threw one leg around Barry's body. She wrapped her arms around his furry neck. And a few minutes later the St. Bernard padded slowly into the courtyard of the monastery with the little girl riding on his back!

Stories like this soon made Barry famous on both sides of the mountains. Barry just went on doing his job. He did it for more than twelve years. And during that time he helped save the lives of 42 people.

But the work was hard and the

weather was harsh. Soon after Barry's
twelfth birthday the monks noticed that
the dog was growing stiff and slow.

Most old dogs were sent to homes in
the warmer valleys below. But the
monks couldn't bear to part with Barry.
So he stayed at the monastery for several more years.

Then winter came once more. One wild and stormy night Barry was sleeping by the fire. There was a lull in the storm. The monks heard nothing. But Barry's ears were still sharp. Suddenly he was wide awake. He moved to the door and began to whine.

The monks thought he wanted to go into the courtyard. But when they opened the door Barry dashed away into the night.

Not far away Barry found what he was looking for — a man lying face downward in the snow. The man must have shouted a few minutes before. But now he lay very still with his eyes closed.

Barry bent over him. The man rolled over. He half opened his eyes. And what he saw made him scream. A big, dim shape was looming over him! "It's a wolf!" the man thought. With the last of his strength he pulled out his knife — and stuck it deep into Barry's side. Then he fainted again.

The old dog was badly wounded. But

he still had a job to do. Somehow Barry got back to the monastery. He sank to the ground. And the monks, lanterns held high, followed his paw prints — and drops of blood — back to the man.

They were in time to save the man's life. But no one was happy at the monastery that night. The monks took turns looking after Barry. At first they thought he would surely die. But finally he grew a little stronger.

Barry grew stronger, but he was never really well again. And he died a few months later.

The monks and the big St. Bernards still live in the high mountains of Switzerland. But life at the monastery is very different now. Far below, a tunnel goes through the mountain. And a safe road has been built through the pass nearby.

So the dogs are no longer needed for rescue work. But Barry has not been forgotten. Every few years an especially lively and intelligent pup is born at the monastery. He is always named Barry.

Balto,
the dog who saved Nome

"THIS IS NOME, ALASKA. REPEAT.
THIS IS NOME, ALASKA. WE NEED
HELP. FAST . . ."

A man bent over the machine in the
Nome telegraph office. Again and again
he pressed down the signal key. *Click-
click-clack . . . Clack-click-clack . . .* He was
sending a message to the town of Anchorage, Alaska, 800 miles to the south.
Click-click-clack . . . Clack-click-clack
. . . The Anchorage telegraph operator

wrote down the message. The news was very bad.

A terrible sickness had broken out in the Nome area — a disease called diphtheria. Some people had already died of it. Many more would die if they weren't treated soon.

There was no medicine to treat diphtheria in Nome. The medicine they needed would have to come from Anchorage — 800 miles away — through a wild wind and snow storm. The storm was so bad that airplanes couldn't fly through it. Trains couldn't get through either. Nome was very near the sea, but the sea was frozen solid. And the road from the south was completely blocked by deep drifts of snow.

There was only one way to get the medicine from Anchorage to Nome — by dogsled.

The medicine was packed in a box and sent north by train — as far as a train could go on the snowy tracks. It was still more than 600 miles south of Nome. From now on teams of dogs would have to take it the rest of the way.

The teams were ready. The first team pushed north through the storm to a little town. There a second team was waiting. It went on to another small town where a third team was ready to take the medicine on north.

At first the teams managed to go many miles before they grew tired. But the storm was growing worse by the minute. Finally Charlie Olson's team staggered into the little village of Bluff — 60 miles south of Nome. They had only gone 20 miles, yet Olson and the dogs were almost frozen and completely worn out.

Gunnar Kasson and his team were waiting in Bluff. The wind screamed through the little town. The snow was piling up deeper and deeper on the ground. It was 30 degrees *below* zero

Fahrenheit outside now. And the temperature was falling fast.

"It's no use trying to go out in *that*," Charlie Olson said. "I almost didn't make it. You and the dogs will freeze solid before you get half way."

But Kasson knew how important the medicine was. He knew that hundreds — maybe thousands — of people would die if they didn't get the medicine soon. Besides, he knew he didn't have to go all the way. Another team was waiting 40 miles north in the little village of Safety. That team would take the medicine the last 20 miles to Nome.

Quickly Gunnar Kasson hitched up his team of dogs. And at the head of the long line he put his lead dog, Balto.

Balto was a mixed-breed. He was half Eskimo dog — and half wolf. Many dogs who are part wolf never become tame. They never learn to trust people — or obey them either. Balto was different. He was a gentle dog who obeyed orders quickly. He also knew how to think for himself.

Usually Gunnar Kasson guided the dogs. He told them where to go. Now he couldn't even see his hand in front of his face. So everything was up to Balto. The big black dog would have to find the trail by smell. Then he'd have to stay on it no matter what happened.

Gunnar Kasson climbed onto the back of the sled. He cracked his whip in the air. *"Mush!"* he cried. *"Move out!"*

The first part of the trail to Nome led across the sea ice. This ice wasn't anything like ice on a small pond or lake. It seemed much more *alive*. And no wonder. The water *under* the ice was moving up and down because of the storm. So the ice was moving up and down too. Up and down, up and down it went, like a roller coaster.

In some places the ice was smooth — as smooth and slippery as glass. Dogs are usually sure-footed. But they slipped and skidded across this ice. So did the sled.

And sometimes the ice came to sharp points — points that dug deep into the dogs' paws.

Worst of all were the places where the ice was bumpy — so bumpy that the sled turned over again and again. Each time it turned over the other dogs began to bark and snap at each other. But Balto always stood quietly while Kasson set the sled upright again. Balto was calm, so the other dogs grew calmer too.

The team had been moving across the ice for hours. Suddenly there was a loud *cracking* sound — like a gun going off. Kasson knew that sound. It was the sound of ice breaking. Somewhere not far ahead the ice had split apart. If the team kept going straight they would run right into the freezing water — and drown.

Balto heard the ice crack too. He slowed for a moment. Then he turned left. He headed straight out to sea. He went for a long time. Then he turned right once more.

Balto was leading the team *around* the icy water. Finally he gave a sharp bark and turned north. He had found the trail to Nome again.

Soon the trail left the sea ice. From now on it was over land. Things should have been easier. They weren't. The snow was falling thick and fast. In some places the wind swept most of it off the trail. But in other places the snow drifts came up almost over the dogs' heads. And the wind was blowing harder and harder. It sent bits of icy snow straight into Kasson's eyes. "I might as well have been blind," he said. "I couldn't even *guess* where we were."

And the dogs were so tired! Again and again they tried to stop. They wanted to lie down and go to sleep in the snow. Balto was just as tired. But he would not stop. He kept on pulling — and the other dogs had to follow behind.

Now something else began to worry Gunnar Kasson. They had been traveling for about 14 hours. Surely they should have reached the town of Safety in 14 hours. Kasson went on for another hour. Then he knew. Somehow they had missed the town in the storm. They must have passed right by the new dog team!

Kasson knew they couldn't stop and wait for the storm to die down. He and the dogs would freeze if they did. They couldn't go back to Bluff either. They had come too far. There was only one thing to do now. Pray . . . and push on to Nome.

Later Gunnar Kasson said he couldn't remember those last miles very well. Each one was a nightmare of howling wind and swirling snow and bitter cold. But somehow — with Balto leading slowly and steadily — they made it! At 5:30 in the morning, February 2, 1925 —

after 20 hours on the trail — the team limped into Nome!

The whole town was waiting for the medicine! They gathered around Gunnar Kasson. They shook his hand and pounded him on the back. "How can we ever thank you?" one woman cried.

Gunnar Kasson shook his head. Then he sank to his knees beside Balto. He began to pull long splinters of ice from the dog's paws. "Balto, what a dog," he

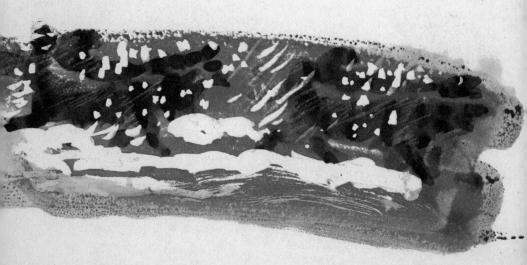

said. "I've been in Alaska for 20 years and this was the toughest trip I've ever made. But Balto, *he* brought us through."

Many newspaper and magazine stories were written about Balto. His picture was printed on postcards and in books. And today, on a grassy hill in New York City's Central Park, there is a life-sized statue of Balto — the dog who saved Nome.

BALTO